MAVIS

& Her Marvelous Mooncakes

written & illustrated by

Dar Hosta

Brown Dog Books
Flemington, New Jersey

Other Books By Dar Hosta
I Love The Night
I Love The Alphabet

Dar's Art Site **www.darsart.com**

First Edition
Copyright © 2006 by Dar Hosta

ISBN-10: 0-9721967-2-2 ISBN-13: 978-0-972196-72-7
LCCN: 2006904699

Published by Brown Dog Books
PO Box 2196 Flemington, NJ 08822
www.browndogbooks.com

The illustrations in this book were created using collage.
The type is Century Gothic. The display type is Samba.

Printed in China

For Ethan & Caleb
My little sugar stars...

If I were to tell you
the moon is a cake
made by a sweet, orange cat...

If I were to tell you
it's delicious with tea,
what would you think of that?

In a happy little house, on a grassy green hill,
by a gentle blue lake, on the sunny side of town,
lives a striped orange cat whose name is
Miss Mavis Sugar.

And when Miss Mavis Sugar is stirring up something sweet in her kitchen, you will always smell something good. Mavis is everyone's favorite baker. Tell me, says Miss Mavis, what might *your* favorite be?

Is it lemon linzers or ladyfingers, whoopie pies or chocolate crinkles?
Is it butter crisps with caramel bits, or vanilla tortes with rainbow sprinkles?

Oh, tell me, tell me, what might *your* favorite be?

Is it jam jubilees or jelly jumbles, apple cobblers with walnut crumbles? Is it brownies or blondies, or seashell sandies, or cocoa drops with cherry candies?

Oh, tell me, tell me, tell me, what might *your* favorite be?

Is it raspberry puffs or snickerdoodles, fudgy buttons or spiced plum strudels? Is it maple yum-yums with butterscotch twirls, or chocolate spritzles with blueberry swirls? What, oh, what? What in the world, might *your* favorite be?

Hooray! Hooray! Her friends all say. It's true they love them all!

But, after a dark and moonless night, Miss Mavis is up with the sun mixing up something *very, very* special.

On a day like today, do you know what you will hear her say?

Mooncake, mooncake
is so nice. I'll make one sweet
and shining slice.

*Something sure smells
good!*

When friends come by for yummy in the tummy smells, make you come a running smells, what do you think she says?

Mooncake, mooncake is so nice.
I'll make one *more* sweet, shining slice!

Buttercreams and sweet moonbeams, starry sprinkles and tasty twinkles. For fourteen days and fourteen nights, what do you think she says?

Mooncake, mooncake is so nice.
I'll make one *more* sweet, shining slice!

With mixing bowls and wooden spoons, these are busy days for a growing moon. This mooncake is getting bigger and bigger and bigger, until one dark and starry night...

Hooray! Hooray! Her friends all say.
It's true the cake is done!

The only thing nicer than a great big
mooncake is having good friends to
share it with. Mavis grins from ear to
ear and what do you think she says?

Mooncake, mooncake is so nice. Now, go ahead and
eat a slice! And the cake is deliciously delicious. For fourteen
days and fourteen nights, they gobble it up in smiling bites. Mavis grins
from ear to ear and what do you think she says?

Mooncake, mooncake is so nice.
Yes, go ahead and eat a slice!

With sticky whiskers and happy tunes, these are delicious nights for a dwindling moon. This mooncake is getting smaller and smaller and smaller, until one dark and starry night...

There is just one thin and shining sliver of mooncake left, and do you know what Miss Mavis says?

Mooncake, mooncake *is* so nice, I think *I'll* eat this last sweet slice!

And the mooncake is marvelously marvelous!

Steamy cups of apple tea, good night stories and snuggle-buggers. Clean, scrubbed faces and soft pajamas, kitty kisses and bedtime huggers. Time to tuck in the sweetie-pies, in the happy little house, on a grassy green hill, by a gentle blue lake, on the sleepy side of town, where a striped orange cat whose name is Miss Mavis Sugar, is thinking of the dark, moonless night.

Magic blankies and brown, big teddies,
dream time comes to cozy beddies.

Sweet dreams, my little sugar stars.
And their dreams are always so very *sweetly sweet*.
Oh, good, Good Night.

OUR MOON

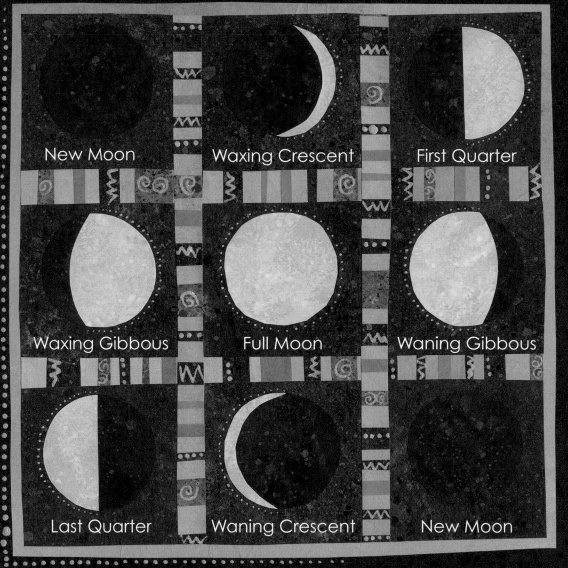

New Moon   Waxing Crescent   First Quarter

Waxing Gibbous   Full Moon   Waning Gibbous

Last Quarter   Waning Crescent   New Moon

It takes 28 days for the Moon to go from New to Full and back to New again.
The Moon has no light of its own, but instead reflects the light of the Sun.
The Moon is not actually round, but egg-shaped.
The same side of the Moon always faces the Earth.
The Moon has no atmosphere, no wind, and no rain.
The Moon is covered with pits and dents that are called *craters*.
The gravity between the Earth and the Moon causes our ocean tides.
It takes about four entire days to travel from the Earth to the Moon in a rocket.